M000107193

Lucy Llama and Friends

Short Stories, Fuzzy Animals, and Life Lessons

Norma MacDonald

Karma for Kids Books

Lucy Llama and Friends
Short Stories, Fuzzy Animals, and Life Lessons

Copyright © 2016 Norma MacDonald

First Edition

Published by: Find Your Way Publishing, Inc.
PO BOX 667
Norway, ME 04268 U.S.A.
www.findyourwaypublishing.com

All rights reserved. No part of this book may be reproduced, stored in a retrieval system or transmitted in any form or by any means, electronic, mechanical, photocopying, recording, or otherwise, without the written permission of the publisher.

ISBN-13: 978-1-945290-00-8

ISBN-10: 1-945290-00-5

Library of Congress Control Number: 2016938859

Printed in the United States of America.

Dedication

This book is dedicated to all of the people trying to make the world a better place. You are making a positive difference!

"You REAP what You SOW: Life is like a boomerang. Our thoughts, deeds and words return to us sooner or later, with astounding accuracy." ~ Grant M. Bright

Table of Contents

About This Book

Welcome to our Karma for Kids Books Series. We are very grateful that you picked up this book. We believe together we can make a positive difference, one child at a time. We strive to instill important life lessons in the lives of young children. We are firm believers in Karma and think that if this simple Law of the Universe is taught to children at a young age, their lives will have the potential to be absolutely amazing.

We once knew a dog named Karma. She was a beautiful, yellow Labrador retriever. It wasn't until after she passed, at 11 years old (God bless her loyal soul.), that we realized just how fitting her name really was.

Karma is indeed a retriever.

Whatever we threw out, Karma was always happy to bring it back to us. It didn't matter what it was, she always brought it back. If we threw out garbage, she'd bring it back without question. If we threw out the most beautiful dog toy, she'd bring it back. It's the same in life. Whatever you send out, is what you will get back. Guaranteed. Every time. Our Karma for Kids Book Series hopes to instill this easy-to-understand Law of the Universe into the lives of children at a young age. The Universe wants to happily bring you all that your heart desires, and it will, effortlessly. But first, you've got to throw out what you want it to bring back to you so that it can! Have fun with this and watch the magic happen. God bless!

Find all of Norma MacDonald's Karma for Kids Books at Amazon.com.

For more of our Karma for Kids books please visit us at:

www.karmaforkidsbooks.wordpress.com
or
www.findyourwaypublishing.com

Other books that we recommend to help children learn important life lessons:

Ethan Eagle and Friends: Short Stories, Fuzzy Animals, and Life Lessons by Norma MacDonald

Billy Brown Bear and Friends: Short Stories, Fuzzy Animals, and Life Lessons by Norma MacDonald

Humble Heron and Friends: Short Stories, Fuzzy Animals, and Life Lessons by Norma MacDonald

Peter Penguin and Friends: Short Stories, Fuzzy Animals and Life Lessons by Norma MacDonald

Guaranteed Success for Kindergarten; 50 Easy Things You Can Do Today! by Marrae Kimball

Guaranteed Success for Grade School; 50 Easy Things You Can Do Today! by Marrae Kimball

The Secret Combination to Middle School: Real Advice from Real Kids, Ideas for Success, and Much More! by Marrae Kimball

Thank you!

Lucy Llama and Friends

Short Stories, Fuzzy Animals, and Life Lessons

Norma MacDonald

Karma for Kids Books

NORMA MACDONALD

Chapter One

The Lost Tooth

LUCY LLAMA WOKE UP one morning and her tooth was loose! She ran to the mirror and wiggled it. She ran to her mother and wiggled it. She ran to her father and wiggled it. Then she ran all the way to school to wiggle it for her friends. Knowing that she would lose her first tooth soon and that the tooth fairy would come visit was exciting.

"Look! Look!" Lucy Llama shouted, "This is the first loose tooth I've had!"

Helga Hippo ran over to look.

Steven Snail ran over to look.

Even Ethan Eagle ran over to look.

"Wow! That is so cool. That means the tooth fairy will come when you lose it!" Helga Hippo said. She had lost her first tooth just last week and came in the next day with a quarter that the tooth fairy left in place of her baby tooth. Lucy Llama was looking forward to getting a quarter of her own.

"Yeah well, just because you are losing your teeth now doesn't mean that they will grow back the way you want them to." Ethan Eagle was jealous that he still hadn't lost any teeth. He didn't even have any that were loose.

"I just can't wait for the tooth fairy to come!" Lucy Llama jumped up and down at the thought of a fairy coming into her room to take her little llama tooth and leave her with a shiny coin.

"Good morning class. Everyone, please take your seats so that we can begin today's lesson!" Mr. Beaver stood at the front of the classroom with a piece of chalk in his hand. When everyone took their seats at their desks, he started to write notes on the chalkboard.

Lucy Llama was too excited to take notes. She sat at her desk wiggling her tooth back and forth all morning until the lunch bell rang.

At the lunch table, everyone was talking about the lesson that Mr. Beaver taught them that morning in class.

"Isn't it so cool that trees sort of breath the opposite way we do? If we didn't have trees around then we wouldn't have oxygen," said Steven Snail. He really loved learning about plants.

Lucy Llama didn't want to talk about nature, she wanted to talk more about her loose tooth. She just couldn't help herself. She was so excited.

"When do you think it will fall out?" She asked her friends.

"I don't know Lucy Llama; didn't you just find out this morning that it was loose? Mine took a week of being loose before it fell out," Helga Hippo said.

"And how cool is it that trees lose their leaves in the fall and then in the winter they look dead, but they aren't?!" Steven Snail was still talking about trees.

"Do you think the tooth fairy will bring me a quarter too?" Lucy Llama asked.

Everyone looked at her. They were starting to get a little bit annoyed.

"Well she gave Helga Hippo a quarter so it wouldn't really be fair if you got more or less," said Ethan Eagle.

They all went back to talking about trees, but Lucy Llama wasn't listening to them. She wiggled and wiggled her tooth hoping that the more she wiggled it the sooner it would fall out.

At recess, all of Lucy Llama's friends were playing a game of tag, but Lucy didn't want to play. She wanted to sit on a bench and watch so that she had some more time to wiggle her tooth.

After school Lucy Llama ran home to her mirror. She stood in front of the mirror wiggling her loose tooth until her mom and dad called her to come to the kitchen table for dinner.

"We made soup for dinner because it won't bother your loose tooth," said her father.

"I just hope it falls out soon!"

Lucy Llama slurped down her soup as fast as she could so that she could go back to her mirror and play with her loose tooth. She loved the idea that her teeth were sort of like trees. Trees lost their leaves for the winter and then grew new ones for the spring and kids lost their teeth as they got older and then grew new ones.

The next day at school, Steven Snail had a loose tooth too! Lucy Llama was a little disappointed that the attention was off of her and now onto Steven, but she was excited that she, at least, had someone to talk to about her teeth!

"Mine wiggles when I breathe in and out like this," Steven Snail announced and he began to whistle showing that his tooth moved back and forth when he did so. "Try it!" He encouraged Lucy Llama.

The two friends sat together all day wiggling their teeth and talking about when they might fall out. Lucy Llama predicted that her tooth would fall out first since it was loose first, and Steven Snail really hoped she was wrong.

After school Steven Snail, Ethan Eagle, and Helga Hippo all went over to play at Lucy Llama's house. In her backyard, they were throwing a football around and playing keep away from Ethan.

He was running around between all three of them trying to intercept passes.

"You'll never get the ball, Ethan!" Lucy Llama was sticking her tongue out at him and mocking him in good fun.

Unfortunately, she did not see that Steven Snail had tossed the ball in her direction but when she saw it coming, it was too late. The ball hit her right in the mouth and it knocked her tooth out!

"Ouch! Steven Snail why did you do that?"

Steven Snail ran over to see if she was okay. "I'm sorry Lucy Llama, I thought you knew it was coming to you! Are you okay?"

"Yes, but you knocked my tooth out!" Lucy Llama looked down to see where her tooth had fallen, but the grass was so tall it made it hard to see anything that small. "My tooth is missing!" Lucy Llama started to panic. How would the tooth fairy know to come to her house if there was no tooth to put under her pillow?!

Everyone ran over to see the new gap in Lucy Llama's smile.

"Wow! You lost your first tooth!" Helga Hippo cheered.

"But it's missing! I don't know where it fell! Steven Snail knocked it out!"

"We will help you find it" Steven Snail promised.

All the friends got down on their hands and knees to look for the lost tooth. They all combed through the grass like they were looking for four leaf clovers. They started to back up to expand the area they were searching.

"It couldn't have gone that far," said Ethan Eagle.

"I don't know, the ball hit Lucy Llama in the face pretty hard," said Helga Hippo.

"What if we don't find it?!"

"Just keep looking everyone!" Said Steven Snail. He felt very bad that he made Lucy Llama lose her tooth. He knew how much she was looking forward to putting her tooth under the pillow for the tooth fairy.

They continued to brush through the grass searching for a little white baby tooth. Lucy Llama was beginning to feel helpless.

"Here!" Ethan Eagle held something in the air triumphantly. Everyone rushed over to see the tooth, but after a closer look, they all realized that it was just a pebble.

"That's not funny Ethan Eagle!" Lucy Llama scolded him, but before she could get really mad, something on the ground caught her eye. It looked like the pebble that Ethan Eagle was holding in his hand, but it was whiter.

She reached down and picked it up and it was her tooth!

All of the friends cheered and Lucy Llama knew that she had great friends because of their efforts. She couldn't wait to tell them what the tooth fairy brought her the next day.

Chapter Two

Hold Mommy's Hand

ETHAN EAGLE HATED WHEN his mom held his hand. He thought he was too old for that. Whenever they went out his mom would say, "Hold mommy's hand." She would extend her wing and make him hold on.

When they crossed streets, she held his hand.

When they were in the grocery store, she held his hand.

When they were in the park, she held his hand.

Ethan Eagle didn't like feeling like a little kid anymore. He wanted to be treated like one of the grown-ups. It made him feel embarrassed that his mom always was holding his hand. He didn't want his friends to see.

On the weekends, Mrs. Eagle liked to go to the local farmer's market to buy fresh fruits and vegetables. It was always a family outing.

"Time to wake up Ethan," she chirped, "we are going to the farmer's market!"

"I don't want to go today," said Ethan Eagle. He was dreading having to hold his mother's hand the whole time.

"Well, you sure can't stay home alone. You're too young for that!"

Ethan Eagle rolled his eyes. He thought that staying home alone would be just fine. Besides, all he wanted to do was stay in bed and watch TV. But Mrs. Eagle wasn't having it. She made Ethan get out of bed and get dressed to go to the farmer's market.

He put a hat on his head, to cover his face, just in case he ran into anyone he knew and wanted to hide. None of his friends still had to hold their mother's hands, at least, he didn't think so.

When they left the house Ethan Eagle was determined to make it through the day without having to hold his mother's hand. If he wasn't allowed to stay home alone he wanted to, at least, be grown up enough to not hold her hand.

They walked to the park and when it came time to cross the busy road into the crowded farmer's market, Mrs. Eagle extended her wing.

"Ethan Eagle, it is time hold mommy's hand," she said.

"I don't want to." Ethan Eagle crossed his wings.

"If you don't hold mommy's hand we could get separated and you could get lost!"

"I'm not a baby anymore, mom!" Ethan Eagled whined.

When there was a break in the traffic, Mrs. Eagle went to grab Ethan's hand to cross the street, but Ethan Eagle took off without her. He ran right across the street and into the busy market. He wanted to prove that he didn't need to hold her hand to get across the street safely.

The crowd of people, who were also crossing the street, consumed and crowded him and before he knew it, Ethan Eagle couldn't see where his mom went. Once he was across safely, he looked around, but she was nowhere in sight!

She is probably just in the farmer's market waiting for me, he thought.

So Ethan Eagle walked confidently into the park with the crowd looking at the tables filled with fresh fruits and vegetables. He walked down the first aisle of tables and didn't find his mom.

I guess I should try the next aisle, he thought, and he looped around to walk down the next line of tables. Ethan Eagle was trying to walk through the market like he knew exactly what he was looking for on the tables, he didn't want to look lost.

"Hey there Ethan Eagle, where is your mother?" Asked one of the vendors.

"We decided to split up," Ethan Eagle lied.

"It's so great that you are helping your mother pick up her fresh produce!" Said the vendor.

Ethan Eagle nodded, but he was starting to get a little worried that he couldn't find his mother. He was afraid that she might leave the market without him and then he would be stranded. He wasn't completely sure how to get home from this park.

After he walked up and down the aisles one more time, Ethan really started to panic. He looked left and he looked right. His mom was nowhere in sight and he didn't know what to do. He really didn't like this feeling. Where could she be? He tried to remember if she wanted to buy anything specific today so he would know exactly where to look, but his thoughts were interrupted by someone shouting his name.

"Ethan Eagle! Hey! Ethan Eagle!"

Ethan Eagle turned to see who the voice was coming from. Mr. Beaver, his teacher from school, was walking toward him. Ethan Eagle tried to look confident, he didn't want his teacher to know that anything was wrong.

"Good morning, Mr. Beaver."

"Are you here at the market all alone?"

"No sir," said Ethan Eagle, "I'm here with my mother. She just walked away for a quick second."

Mr. Beaver nodded. "Well Ethan Eagle, I just ran into your mother at the entryway of the park. She seemed very worried that she didn't know where you were."

Ethan Eagle was so excited to hear that his mother was still there. "You saw my mom?!" He couldn't hide his excitement. "I've been looking for her everywhere! Please tell me where she is!"

Mr. Beaver smiled, "Why don't I walk you over to where she is. Or are you grown up enough to walk over there on your own?"

Ethan Eagle really wanted to go over on his own to prove that he could be a grown up but he didn't want to risk getting lost in the market again. He hadn't thought that they would get separated in the first place. Now, he just wanted to find his mom. He said, "It would be nice if you took me over to her, please."

Mr. Beaver led the way and Ethan Eagle followed him to the front of the park.

When Ethan Eagle saw his mom waiting there, he noticed that she looked very worried. When she saw him, she ran over and gave him a big hug.

"You had me so worried Ethan!"

"I'm sorry mom!" said Ethan Eagle, He was so happy, that he almost started to cry. "I should have listened to you and held your hand! I didn't mean to get lost, but there were so many others and I lost you in the crowd! Now I know why it's important to hold onto your hand."

Mrs. Eagle was so happy that she was reunited with her son. She knew that he was very sorry that he hadn't listened about holding her hand, so she didn't yell at him. She just said, "if that ever happens again, just stay where you last saw me and we will find each other easier than if we are just both wandering around." It was punishment enough that he was so scared that he couldn't find her, she knew that Ethan learned his lesson.

"I promise," Ethan Eagle said. He knew that he would never disobey his mom again.

Chapter Three

The Community Garden

STEVEN SNAIL LOVES trees and flowers and all sorts of other plants. His favorite activity was going on hikes through the woods.

It made Steven Snail very sad to see that some of his favorite places to explore in the woods had been chopped down and turned into buildings. He wanted to do something to help the earth.

Steven Snail decided that the best thing he could do was start a community garden. Instead of building more houses on the land, he would build a garden so that more trees and flowers and other plants could grow.

He started off by asking his friends for help.

"Do you want to help me plant some trees?" Steven Snail asked Helga Hippo.

"I'm too busy today. I have to do my homework," she said.

"Do you want to come plant flowers with me?" Steven Snail asked Lucy Llama.

"I'm too busy today. I have to do my chores," she said.

"Do you want to garden with me today?" Steven Snail asked Ethan Eagle.

"I'm too busy today. I have to go somewhere with my mom," he said.

So Steven Snail set off alone. First, he went to the flower store. At the flower store, he bought four packets of seeds. A packet of tulip seeds, a packet of sunflower seeds, a packet of rose seeds, and a packet of daffodil seeds.

Next, Steven Snail went to the tree store. He bought a small oak tree seed, a small pine tree seed, and a small maple tree seed.

Then Steven Snail took the seeds all back to the community garden. No one had used the garden in a very long time, so Steven Snail needed to clean it up. He ripped all the weeds out of the ground so that it would look pretty. Then he raked the soil to loosen it up, this way it would be easier to dig holes for the seeds.

After he got the garden ready, he started to dig holes.

"Hey, Steven Snail," someone across the street called, "what are you doing?"

Steven Snail looked up and saw Mr. and Mrs. Hippo across the street.

"I am planting new things in the garden. I think it is important that this city has some nature in it!"

"What a great idea," said Mr. Hippo.

"We should send Helga over to help," said Mrs. Hippo.

They walked off, and not too long later, Helga Hippo arrived in the garden.

"Hi, Steven Snail. My mom and dad said that I should come over here and help you plant things in the community garden."

"Great!" Steven Snail said, "you can start watering all the seeds I just put in the ground!"

Helga Hippo picked up the watering bucket and followed Steven Snail around the garden. She poured water on each pile of dirt covering the seeds.

"Why are you doing this?" Helga Hippo asked.

"Because plants are important to nature, don't you remember the lesson we learned in class the other day?"

Helga Hippo shrugged and said, "Yeah, but it's not your job to plant the trees. Gardeners can do that. And if you are the only one, then will it make a difference?"

"I'm not the only one," said Steven Snail, "You're helping too!"

The next day Steven Snail and Helga Hippo walked to the garden together to water the seeds. It still just looked like a big old pile of dirt, but Steven Snail knew that in a few days green leaves would be sprouting up out of the ground.

"Where are you guys going?" Lucy Llama called out after them one day while they were walking to the garden.

"We are going to water our plants in the garden!" Helga Hippo called out.

"Come with us!" Steven Snail said.

Lucy Llama trotted up next to them and followed them to the garden.

"There is nothing here," said Lucy Llama.

"Not yet!" Steven Snail said.

"After we keep watering the seeds and pulling out the bad plants, which are weeds, then our plants will bloom," said Helga Hippo, "just wait!"

With three friends helping to keep the garden looking nice and the plants watered, things went a lot faster. And they had more time to play after taking care of all the seeds.

One their way home from the garden, they ran into Ethan Eagle.

"Where were you guys?" Ethan Eagle asked.

"We were being gardeners!" Lucy Llama said.

"That sounds boring," said Ethan Eagle.

The three friends ignored that Ethan Eagle was being negative. He often liked to act like he was too cool, but they knew that once the plants bloomed, Ethan would want to be a part of the garden.

After another couple of days tending to the community garden, the first bits of green began popping out of the ground all over the place.

"Look!" Steven Snail shouted, "The oak tree is blooming!"

"And so are all the roses!" Helga Hippo shrieked.

"All of the plants are starting to grow! We did it!" Lucy Llama cheered.

They jumped up and down and exchanged high fives to congratulate each other on their hard work. While they were celebrating, Ethan Eagle came by.

"What's going on?" He asked.

"All of the plants are finally growing!" Steven Snail announced.

Ethan Eagle thought it was pretty cool that they made something grow where nothing was before. He decided that he would help them tend the garden.

In school, the four friends won the green thumb award for bringing the community garden back to life again and for helping to keep their city beautiful. With a little bit of effort, a big mound of dirt became a beautiful garden for all to enjoy.

NORMA MACDONALD

Chapter Four

Try It

HELGA HIPPO WAS A very picky eater. She didn't like food that was green, she didn't like fruits, and she didn't like sandwiches. All Helga Hippo ate was cheese and crackers and carrots. Whenever her friends were eating something at lunch time that looked weird, she decided that was another food she didn't like.

One day Lucy Llama was eating celery and Helga Hippo announced, "That looks disgusting. That's why I don't eat green food."

Another day Steven Snail was eating an orange and when he peeled it juice squirted out. Helga Hippo cried out, "Your food just spit at me. I don't like food that spits at me. That's why I don't eat fruits!"

Even when Ethan Eagle was eating a brownie, Helga Hippo got grossed out that it left chocolate on his fingers, so she said, "brownies are gross. I don't like them."

Poor Mr. Hippo and Mrs. Hippo had a hard time deciding what to make for dinner every night because they weren't sure if their daughter would even eat the meal.

She didn't eat the caesar salad because the lettuce was too green. She didn't eat the sweet potatoes because only candy should taste sweet. She didn't eat the eggplant because she had never seen a purple vegetable before. She didn't eat the spaghetti squash because it didn't know if it was spaghetti or squash.

"Just try it," said Helga Hippo's mother.

"You might like it," said Helga Hippo's father.

Helga Hippo poked the food with her fork and wrinkled her nose. "Can I just have cheese and crackers?"

Helga Hippo ate cheese and crackers for dinner for the third night in a row. Her parents just didn't know how to make her try new food!

They tried having her close her eyes and try new food, but she didn't trust them. "You're going to make me eat a fruit!"

Even at lunch when her friends were eating their favorite foods she wouldn't try it no matter how many times they said it tasted amazing. Helga Hippo refused to try anything she thought might not taste good.

One day Helga Hippo was invited to Steven Snail's birthday party. It was at a pizza place. Helga Hippo liked pizza because it was pretty much just bread and cheese. So she decided to go to the party and eat the pizza with all of her friends.

Steven Snail wanted to try a new kind of pizza so he ordered one with broccoli on it and one with ham and pineapple on it.

Helga Hippo's eyes got big with surprise when she saw the two pizza pies.

"Why is there fruit on the pizza?!" Helga Hippo shrieked.

"It's called Hawaiian pizza," said Steven Snail.

"It's so good!" Ethan Eagle said as he was taking a huge bite from his slice.

Helga Hippo decided that pizza with fruit on it was too weird so she looked at the other pizza.

"Why is there broccoli on the pizza?!" She shrieked.

"Because that's my favorite vegetable!" Steven Snail said with a big smile as he grabbed a piece of broccoli pizza.

"Green food is disgusting!"

All of the friends at the birthday party were ignoring Helga Hippo's complaints. Everyone's mouth was filled with pizza and no one was whining about how it tasted. Helga felt sort of left out that no one else thought the idea of broccoli and fruit on pizza was weird. Everyone else was eating it and seemed to really enjoy it. Some were even going for seconds.

Maybe it isn't that bad, Helga thought.

She took a piece of the Hawaiian pizza with ham and pineapple on it. At least, it isn't green, she thought.

No one was even paying attention to the fact that she was about to try something new. She took a little tiny bite off the tip of the slice she was holding. She got nothing but cheese and it tasted like normal pizza. Helga Hippo knew that one bite wasn't enough, she was really hungry!

Everyone was now going for their third slice of pizza. If Helga Hippo didn't eat her pizza now, there might not be enough food left for her. She took another bite, this time, it had a piece of pineapple on it.

Helga Hippo chewed tentatively waiting for the disgusting taste to take over and make her spit the pizza out, but that didn't happen! She was so surprised at the sweet taste and that she was actually enjoying the pizza.

"Hey Helga Hippo, are you eating pizza with fruit on it?" Lucy Llama called out to her.

"Yeah," Helga Hippo said, "and it doesn't even taste gross!"

All of her friends cheered that Helga Hippo finally tried something new. For dessert Steven Snail made her try his birthday brownies and she liked those too!

When Helga Hippo went home from Steven Snail's birthday pizza party she was so excited to tell her mom and dad that she tried new food. They were very proud of their daughter for finally taking a chance and realizing that even though food might not look good to her, it doesn't mean it can't taste great!

"What's for dinner tomorrow night?" Helga Hippo asked excitedly. "I'm looking forward to trying new foods."

Chapter Five

Count to Ten

SOMETIMES ETHAN EAGLE got very angry about things. During recess, if someone beat him to the swings, he would yell that it wasn't fair, and stomp off mad. If a classmate got a better grade than him on homework, he would complain and say they cheated. Even at home, he would sometimes get mad at his mom if she wanted him to clean his room or help out with dinner.

Ethan Eagle wasn't a mean boy, he just had a bit of a temper.

Mr. Beaver was holding a classroom spelling bee one day and all of the students got to line up and take turns spelling words. If they spelled the word wrong, they had to go back to their desk.

Mr. Beaver announced that the winner didn't have to do the homework assignment that night!

Ethan Eagle really wanted to win the spelling bee. He was a great speller!

Lucy Llama was first.

"Spell the word, laugh," said Mr. Beaver.

"L-A," Lucy Llama paused. She knew that laugh wasn't spelled exactly how it sounded, and she tried to remember the rest of the letters. She started again, "L-A-U-G-H."

"Correct!" Mr. Beaver sent her to the back of the line.

Steven Snail was next.

"Spell the word, though."

Steven Snail spoke quickly and he said, "T-H-O-U."

"I'm sorry Steven Snail, you forgot that there is G-H as the end."

Steven Snail slumped his shoulders and sulked back to his desk to watch the rest of the class participate in the spelling bee.

"Okay Helga Hippo," said Mr. Beaver, "Please spell the word, helpful."

Helga Hippo thought for a second. She could not remember if there were one or two Ls at the end. She went with one. "H-E-L-P-F-U-L."

"Correct!"

Helga Hippo walked triumphantly to the back of the line. Now it was Ethan Eagle's turn. He knew all three of the first words easily. He was confident that he would get the next one too.

"Spell the world, eager."

"E-E-G-E-R!" Ethan Eagle shouted each letter out.

"I'm sorry Ethan Eagle, but eager is actually spelled E-A-G-E-R," said Mr. Beaver, "please take your seat back at your desk."

"That wasn't a fair word! It hasn't been on our vocabulary list yet! How was I supposed to know it was E A and not E E?!" Ethan Eagle was shouting at Mr. Beaver and stomping his feet.

"None of the words today have been on our vocabulary list, Ethan. Please take your seat now so we can continue the spelling bee," said Mr. Beaver.

"This is stupid!" Ethan Eagle swung his wing and knocked the eraser off the ledge on the chalkboard then stomped back to his desk and sat down. He was scowling. Mr. Beaver walked over to him and asked him to take a walk down to the principal's office to cool down.

Ethan Eagle hated being sent to the principal's office. Whenever that happened, the principal would call his mom and then Ethan Eagle would be punished when he got home. As hard as he tried, Ethan Eagle just couldn't control his temper.

Whenever he got mad, he shouted and threw things, he didn't know what else to do.

"What brings you here today, Ethan Eagle?" Mrs. Pidgeon, the principal, asked.

"I got mad that I spelled a word wrong in the class spelling bee and started to shout at Mr. Beaver. But it really wasn't fair!" Ethan Eagle told her.

"It seems like you get mad often, is that true?"

"Yes," said Ethan Eagle.

"How do you try to avoid getting mad? "Principal Pidgeon asked.

Ethan Eagle shrugged. He never really thought about ways to avoid becoming so angry. Usually, he just let it happen. "I just like when things go my way," he said.

"Let's try something," said Principal Pidgeon.

"Are you going to tell my mom I was behaving badly?" Ethan Eagle was worried that when he went home he would have to deal with getting yelled at again.

"If you promise me that you will try a new way to deal with your anger, then I won't call your mom this time. If you act up in class again, though, I will have to call her. Does that sound like a good plan?"

"How will I deal with my anger, though?" Ethan Eagle really wanted to try, but he didn't know how.

"Next time something makes you feel upset or mad or frustrated, I want you to take a deep breath and count to ten before you say anything. Then once you've done that, you can react," said Principal Pidgeon.

"How will counting to ten help me not be mad?" Ethan Eagle asked.

"Just try it."

Ethan Eagle went home that day and told his mom that school was fine. He did his homework, and went to bed. He kept thinking about what Principal Pidgeon told him to do when he felt angry, but he was worried. Counting to ten didn't seem like a good way to keep him from being mad. He didn't see what good that would do.

When he got into the classroom the next day his friends were all talking about the homework assignment. They each had to write a story using the words from the spelling bee. Ethan Eagle tried to tune them out.

"I bet you're eager to share your story, Ethan Eagle," said Lucy Llama. She was making fun of him for misspelling the word eager.

Ethan Eagle felt himself getting upset because he was getting teased by Lucy. He was just about to yell at her for being mean, but he remembered what the Principal Pidgeon told him to do. Ethan Eagle started to count.

One.

Two.

Three.

He started to think that Lucy Llama was just joking. They were friends and that's what friends do.

Four.

Five.

Six.

Lucy Llama didn't know that she was hurting his feelings.

Seven.

Eight.

It won't help anyone if Ethan Eagle yells at her. He might even get in trouble for it. Or worse, get sent to the principal's office again.

Nine.

He should just let her know that he didn't find the joke funny.

Ten.

"Lucy Llama, I was pretty sad that I spelled that word wrong yesterday and I don't think it's nice that you are making a joke about it," said Ethan Eagle.

Lucy Llama was surprised. She said, "I'm sorry Ethan, I was just trying to be funny."

Ethan Eagle felt better. For once he didn't lose his temper! And he was able to deal with his anger in a good way that didn't get him sent to the principal. Counting to ten gave him a chance to think about what he was mad about and how to deal with it. Ethan Eagle was glad that he finally learned how to stay calm, and he actually couldn't wait to try it again. He didn't like getting angry so quickly. It always made him feel bad inside. Now he had a tool to help him!

Chapter Six

It's Okay to Be Unique

LUCY LLAMA LOVED to wear purple velvet vests, but she never wore them to school because it wasn't in style. Instead, she wore normal clothes, a shirt with some sort of design on it and a pair of jeans or a skirt. None of her friends knew that she really loved purple velvet vests because she was too embarrassed to show them her style. They might call her weird.

Steven Snail liked to paint his nails. When he saw his friends who were girls wearing nail polish, he was jealous. He didn't know why it wasn't normal for boys to paint their nails. So he never wore nail polish to school. Instead, he painted his nails on the weekend when he wouldn't see his friends in school. He was worried that if he wore nail polish to school they might call him a girl. He wasn't a girl at all. He just liked how the colors looked on his nails. He liked the bright colored paints the best.

Helga Hippo hated skirts. She thought they were really uncomfortable. She didn't like that she had to always make sure the wind didn't blow her skirt the wrong way and worry that everyone might see her underwear. Helga Hippo wore skirts anyway because she was a girl and girls were supposed to wear skirts sometimes. A lot of the other girls in her school wore skirts, so, so did Helga Hippo. She was afraid that if she didn't wear skirts, her friends might think she wanted to be a boy.

Ethan Eagle listened to show tunes. His favorite movies were musicals where the characters would be in the middle of a conversation and then break out into song. Ethan Eagle knew all the words to the songs to many different musicals. None of his friends knew he listened to show tunes, though, because usually the kids at his school didn't listen to that type of music. He was afraid they might laugh at him.

During class one day, Mr. Beaver asked everyone what made them unique.

"Well, I'm the only llama in class," said Lucy Llama.

"But you aren't the only llama in town," said Mr. Beaver, "Think harder. What is something that is special about you just because it's you?"

"I know how to skateboard," said Steven Snail.

"But so do I," said Helga Hippo.

No one in the class could think of anything that was unique about them that no one else had in common. They were all too afraid to admit what they like to do, in fear that it would make them look weird and not normal.

"It's nice that you all have so much in common," said Mr. Beaver, "but isn't that kind of boring?"

The class agreed.

"Your homework tonight is to think hard about something that only applys to you. For me, it's that I will only wear socks when they are inside out!"

The class laughed at Mr. Beaver's unique fact. The thought of wearing socks inside out was so silly, no one else in the class preferred inside out socks. It reminded Lucy Llama about how much she liked purple velvet vests. It reminded Steven Snail about how he liked to paint his nails. It reminded Helga Hippo that she thought skirts were uncomfortable. It reminded Ethan Eagle that he loved to listen to show tunes.

When Lucy Llama got home from school she put on her favorite purple velvet vest and danced around her room. She looked in the mirror and thought, I think this vest looks awesome. I don't care if other people think it's not in style. Maybe I will be brave tomorrow and wear it to school.

When Steven Snail got home from school he painted his nails bright neon yellow. He looked down and thought, this color is fantastic, I don't care if people think boys shouldn't paint their nails.

When Helga Hippo got home from school she took her skirt off and put on sweatpants. She was so much more comfortable. She thought, I'm never going to wear a skirt again, I don't care if people think that is weird.

When Ethan Eagle got home from school he turned on his cd player and put in his favorite cd. He sang along to all the words of the show tunes. Ethan Eagle thought, these songs are great, I don't care if people think show tunes are only for old people. I like them so much.

Everyone went to sleep and thought about what they were going to tell the class tomorrow about what made them unique. All of the friends were a little nervous that they might be laughed at, but being yourself was more important than being boring.

In school, the next day, everyone had the jitters. Lucy Llama was sitting at her desk, still wearing her coat. She wasn't ready to show everyone her purple velvet vest just yet. Steven Snail was sitting on his hands to hide his painted nails. Helga Hippo was wearing jeans and hoped that no one would say anything. Hopefully, they wouldn't notice until the next day anyway. Ethan Eagle had his headphones in and was trying hard not to sing out loud or let anyone hear his music. He wasn't ready for his friends to know his unique music taste yet.

Mr. Beaver stood up at the front of the classroom and cleared his throat to get everyone's attention. Usually, the class was talkative and rowdy and it took Mr. Beaver a few minutes to quiet them down, but today that wasn't the case.

"Good morning class," said Mr. Beaver.

"Good morning, Mr. Beaver," said the class.

"Well let's get started by going over your homework," said Mr. Beaver, "Who would like to go first?"

No one in the class volunteered. Going first was always a scary place to be, but now that the class was going to talk about what made them unique, they were even more nervous.

"Steven Snail, what about you?" Mr. Beaver asked. Usually, Steven Snail was the most outgoing in the class and volunteered to go first for things, but today was different.

Steven Snail looked around to see if anyone else would volunteer, but no one did.

"Okay," said Steven Snail and he reluctantly walked to the front of the class. Once he got up there he slowly raised his painted nails to show everyone. "I'm unique because I like to paint my nails and most boys don't do that."

"Thank you for sharing!" Mr. Beaver said.

No one laughed at Steven Snail.

Lucy Llama raised her hand and said, "I guess I will go next." She took her coat off to reveal her purple velvet vest. "I'm unique because I really love to wear purple velvet vests. I have six of them!"

"Wonderful!" Mr. Beaver said.

No one laughed at Lucy Llama.

Next, Ethan Eagle walked to the front of the class. He said, "I'm unique because I love show tunes and I know all the words." He turned the volume up so that the class could hear what he was listening to in his headphones.

"That is a great song!" Mr. Beaver said.

No one laughed at Ethan Eagle.

Helga Hippo was the last to go. She walked to the front of the class and said, "I'm unique because most girls like to wear skirts but I think they are really uncomfortable. I decided not to wear them anymore."

"Good for you!" Mr. Beaver said.

No one laughed at Helga Hippo.

"Isn't it so great how different and unique we all are?" Mr. Beaver asked the class.

They all nodded in agreement. It was pretty cool to see how everyone was different in their own ways. Even though Lucy Llama liked to wear stylish clothes, purple velvet vests were stylish to her even if no one else thought so. Even though Steven Snail was a boy, he liked to paint his nails and thought it was silly that only girls did that. Even though Helga Hippo was a girl, she didn't like to wear skirts even though all the other girls did. Even though Ethan Eagle was a kid he liked listening to show tunes with his parents.

None of these things made the friends weird, it just made them unique, and being unique is what keeps things interesting! Being exactly the same as others isn't any fun anyway. How boring would it be if we were all the same? The friends were so happy that they were able to share what made them unique.

•

AFTERWORD

Thanks again for picking up this book! You are participating in making our world a better place.

For more of our Karma for Kids books please visit us at:

www.karmaforkidsbooks.wordpress.com

or

www.findyourwaypublishing.com

Find Norma MacDonald and her books online at Amazon.com.

Ethan the Eagle and Friends; Short Stories, Fuzzy Animals, and Life Lessons by Norma MacDonald

Billy Brown Bear and Friends; Short Stories, Fuzzy Animals, and Life Lessons by Norma MacDonald

Humble Heron and Friends; Short Stories, Fuzzy Animals, and Life Lessons by Norma MacDonald

Peter Penguin and Friends; Short Stories, Fuzzy Animals, and Life Lessons by Norma MacDonald

Other books that we recommend to help children
learn important life lessons:

*Guaranteed Success for Kindergarten; 50 Easy Things
You Can Do Today!* by Marrae Kimball

*Guaranteed Success for Grade School; 50 Easy Things
You Can Do Today!* by Marrae Kimball

*The Secret Combination to Middle School: Real Advice
from Real Kids, Ideas for Success, and Much More!* by
Marrae Kimball

NORMA MACDONALD

If you have ideas for stories, please feel free to share
and send them to:

Melissa Eshleman
Find Your Way Publishing, Inc.
PO Box 667
Norway, ME 04268
Melissa@findyourwaypublishing.com

www.findyourwaypublishing.com

Thank you!

CPSIA information can be obtained
at www.ICGtesting.com
Printed in the USA
FSOW02n0804201216
28748FS

9 781945 290008